constellations

Twenty Years of Stellar Poetry from Polestar

POLESTAR

An Imprint of Raincoast Books

Polestar Books and Raincoast Books gratefully acknowledge the support of the Government of Canada through the Book Publishing Industry Development Program, the Canada Council and the Department of Canadian Heritage. We also acknowledge the assistance of the Province of British Columbia through the British Columbia Arts Council.

Cover photograph by DC Lowe/Stone

National Library of Canada Cataloguing in Publication Data

Constellations

ISBN 1-55192-500-1

1. Canadian poetry (English)—20th century.
PS8293.C649 2001   C811'.5408   C2001-910866-4
PR9195.7.C67 2001

Polestar, an Imprint of Raincoast Books
9050 Shaughnessy Street
Vancouver, British Columbia
Canada   V6P 6E5
www.raincoast.com

1 2 3 4 5 6 7 8 9 10

At Raincoast Books we are committed to protecting the environment and to the responsible use of natural resources. We are acting on this commitment by working with suppliers and printers to phase out our use of paper produced from ancient forests. This book is one step towards that goal. It is printed on 100% ancient-forest-free paper (100% post-consumer recycled), processed chlorine and acid-free, and supplied by New Leaf Paper; it is printed with vegetable-based inks by Friesens. For further information, visit our website at www.raincoast.com. We are working with Markets Initiative (www.oldgrowthfree.com) on this project.

Printed and bound in Canada

To Pablo

In school, I hated poetry — those skinny,
Malnourished poems that professors love;
The bad grammar and dirty words that catch
In the mouth like fishhooks, tear holes in speech.
Pablo, your words are rain I run through,
Grass I sleep in.

— George Elliott Clarke, Whylah Falls

CONTENTS

FOREWORD

In 1981, Luanne Armstrong's *Castle Mountain* rolled off the press in the basement of University of Victoria's Creative Writing Department. It was the first book to be published by Polestar's founder and first publisher, Julian Ross. *Castle Mountain* is a tactile, earthy book, evocative of the environment from which it grew — the west Kootenay region of BC. It marked the beginning of two decades of publishing not only poetry, but also fiction, children's books, hockey titles, regional texts and creative non-fiction. But poetry has always been at the heart of the Polestar mandate. *Castle Mountain* was the first in an impressive collection of poetry as Polestar sought out, worked with and published some of the most important and popular Canadian poets of the past two decades.

The work itself reveals a diversity of experiences and preoccupations, and ranges across time and space. John MacKenzie writes from Prince Edward Island, George Elliott Clarke from the heart of black Nova Scotia; Jim Green's *North Book* evokes the enchanting mystery of the Northwest Territories while *Castle Mountain* honours the Kootenays. Paulette Jiles brings to life the spare, haunting landscape of Jesse James' Missouri while *To This Cedar Fountain*, Kate Braid's homage to Emily Carr, is lush with images of the west coast rainforest.

Perhaps the one constant in the poetry is the attempt to speak honestly and brilliantly to and about *people*, in all our complexity, contradictions, ordinariness and extremes. Polestar has published work that explores other people's experiences (Paulette Jile's *Jesse James Poems* and Kate Braid's *Inward to the Bones*), poetry that tells of personal struggles and triumphs (Kate Braid's *Covering Rough Ground*, Gregory Scofield's *The Gathering*) and poems about the experience of a community or individual struggling against prejudice, racism and internal pressures (Marie Anneharte Baker's *Being on the Moon* and Gregory Scofield's *Native Canadiana*). In George Elliott Clarke's *Whylah Falls* and *Beatrice Chancy*, we witness the poet's creation of a mythic community populated by lovers, murderers, mothers and (of course) poets. Love and its accompanying agonies and ecstasies are explored in Brenda Brooks' *Blue Light In The Dash*, Greg Scofield's *Love Medicine and One Song*, Shani Mootoo's *The Predicament of Or* and Angela Hryniuk's *no visual scars*, while domestic preoccupations cohabit with political concerns in Sandy Shreve's *Bewildered Rituals*, Pat Lowther's *Time Capsule*, David Zieroth's *The Weight of My Raggedy Skin*, Nadine McInnis' *Hand to Hand* and Aislinn Hunter's *Into the Early Hours*.

These days, there is speculation about the fate of the book, about the declining sales of books-on-paper ("page-poetry" is a recent term for poems in book form) even as interest in poetry appears to be increasing. From our perspective inside a publishing house dedicated to discovering new and exciting poetic voices, the trends are difficult to gauge. There *are* new poets who address familiar themes in fresh ways, and there are familiar poets who are continuing to engage readers with vibrant ideas and exciting language. We will continue to seek them out and publish their work. And we'll continue to develop our other books — our similarly diverse and accomplished fiction, our creative non-fiction, our children's books — around that poetic mandate.

It is fitting, then, that we at Polestar mark our twentieth anniversary with *Constellations*, a book that contains a multitude of voices – at least one from each book of poetry we've published. We haven't tried to unite these voices thematically; instead, we hoped they'd form a bright and singular constellation, one that contains a multitude of possibilities to take us into the future.

Thank you to the designers who have helped us to develop such a fine-looking collection of work and thanks to the booksellers who remain committed to putting poetry into the hands of readers. Thanks to our colleagues in the publishing industry, who continue to persevere. Especially, of course, thanks to the poets who remain committed to telling their stories — all of our stories. You define us and remind us who we are.

Michelle Benjamin, Publisher
October, 2001

Luanne Armstrong

*Luanne Armstrong was born and raised on a farm on
the East Shore of Kootenay Lake, and has lived there for most of
her life. She completed a* BFA *in Creative Writing at the University
of Victoria and an* MFA *at the University of British Columbia.
She has taught Creative Writing at the University of Alberta, the
College of the Rockies and the Kootenay School of Arts in Nelson
and was the Berton House writer in residence in Dawson City,
Yukon, from September to December 2000. She is also the
managing editor of Hodgepog Books, which publishes early
chapter books for children.*

*Luanne Armstrong's publication credits include Polestar's
first-ever poetry book,* Castle Mountain *(Polestar, 1981); the
novels* Annie *(Polestar, 1995),* Bordering *(Ragweed Press, 1995)
and* The Colour of Water *(Caitlin Press, 1998); the poetry
chapbook* The Woman in the Garden *(Peachtree Press, 1996);
and three children's books.*

from CASTLE MOUNTAIN (1981)

July

Dowager summer
arrives late, content
with Emeralds and charity —
the garden grows despite the rain
which topples the standing hay
turns peaches and cherries
soggy with fungus
scents the air
with October.
We cultivate promises
as sour and hopeful
as green apples
the kids bite once and leave.
We talk about next year,
harvest peas and spinach
drink our morning coffee
in silence.

I harvest words
each a kernel, a husk,
a promise.

Drought

Burnt grass crackles with wings—
beside the road, white dust
gauzed over dying apple trees.

The pines are copper, stiff with resin
and dry heat.

Before I could remember, this place
held voices,
my grandfather's, my father's,
now mine.
I learned this union with dry earth
this seeking
too young to change now.

I wait.
I want new voices to come
from the broken hill
like water from stone
witching for power
to well up from dust;
the voices of buried gods, barbed
under fences, and plowed earth.

The bracken shimmers on the hill.
Nine generations of sour Scots farmers behind me
never a poet
a heritage of dust.

The osprey whistles above me,
plays all day, sliding the updraft.

Waiting for the Moon to Change

Bitter rind moon
above the torn river.

My sandals whine and creak
along the polished floor

away from the window
and back.

Her thin brown body
tangled
in ivory tubes,

the breathing rhythm
of machines.

Black river under the bridge
slides away from me.

Marie Annharte Baker

Marie Annharte Baker is an Anishinabe poet, teacher and activist. Born in 1942 to Salteaux and Irish parents, and raised in Winnipeg, her poetry combines the rich heritage of Native traditions with the harsh reality of life on the streets. Being on the Moon was her first book. She has also published Blueberry Canoe (New Star, 2001). Marie Annharte Baker lives in Merritt, British Columbia.

Old-Fashioned Indian

Sniffing the country in your hair
burning from the woodstove of your lips
brushing a deer running down one leg
feeling porcupine fingers crawling on me

Holding in me the water rings from a bullfrog
jumping your old fur hide blanket for a night
waking you say someone snored in your back

Coming on to me many times a moon today
an old-fashioned Indian trading treaties
sky, water, grub, one more drink or two

Shacking up the old-fashioned way
saving the church collection
peddling your heart on your trail
moving on to another wedding day

Pretty Tough Skin Woman

old dried out meat piece
preserved without a museum
missing a few big rips
her skin was guaranteed

her bloomers turned grey
outliving the city washing
not enough drinks to keep her
from getting home to the bush

tough she pushed bear fat down
squeezed into sally ann clothes
she covered her horny places
they tried sticking her under

soft jelly spots remain in bone
holding up this pretty tough hide
useful as a decorated shield for baby
swinging in her sweet little stink
just smell her old memories, gutted fish
baked muskrat — she saw a lady
in a shopping mall with a fur coat
told her an Indian must eat such delicacies

her taste was good she just needed a gun
to find a room in the city to put down
her beat-up mattress where her insides fell out
visitors ate up the bannock drank her tea

they were good at hocking her radio or tv
everywhere she stopped she told her troubles
if I press my ear down on this trail I bet
I'll be able to hear her laughing and gabbing

Gypsy Fix

In this no man's land a gypsy fortune teller
promises that for three thousand dollars cash
I will receive total psychic joy.
A bit pricey this alteration of my darker self,
instead I get my truck fixed. Done, feminized.
A farmer had fiddled with her motor one spring
coupling her with an absolutely wrong alternator.
Warned repeatedly it might drop out unexpectedly
as I drove dusty roads I accepted the severity
of her manifold problem and enjoyed greasy men
hanging over her hood talking about her Y pipe
curved and connected under her body nodding to me
their approval while I practised the proper names
a junk dealer needs to find the exact part to fit.

Hooker Moon

Big wads grab her greedy eyes
Small change no tricks worth playing
Cops bother her only she's looking
For her sister living in the north end
Funny address she lost at the last hotel
Couple of twenties stuck in her bra
Cashy night here comes another boozer
She sings Roll With Me Henry Tonight
Share a lodge for a suitcase of beer
Just wiggle into a moss-lined cradle
Handicrafted with quill; lullaby extra
Cosy up mister around her fire
See footprints of her brothers' war dancing

Kate Braid

Kate Braid was born in Calgary, Alberta and now lives in Burnaby, British Columbia. Over the years she has worked as a receptionist, secretary, child-care worker, teacher, lumber piler and carpenter. She has been the Director of the Labour Studies Program at Simon Fraser University and has also taught Creative Writing at the University of British Columbia (UBC), Malaspina College and Capilano College. She completed her Masters degree in Creative Writing at UBC and is a member of the women writers' group, "Sex, Death & Madness." Braid's first book, Covering Rough Ground, *about her experience as a woman carpenter, won the Pat Lowther Award for the best book of poetry by a Canadian Woman.* To This Cedar Fountain *was shortlisted for a BC Book Prize, and Braid's third book,* Inward to the Bones, *won the VanCity Book Prize.*

These Hips

Some hips are made for bearing
children, built like stools
square and easy, right
for the passage of birth.

Others are built like mine.
A child's head might never pass
but load me up with two-by-fours
and watch me
bear.

When the men carry sacks of concrete
they hold them high, like boys.
I bear mine low, like a girl
on small, strong hips
built for the birth
of buildings.

The Sacrament of Wood

Half priest, half peasant
framed
in the sweet smelling ribs
of her own created space,
a carpenter
can mend things, she can
build things but she can't
go inside
all this meaning.

Bending, she serves her creation
as fingers of roof throw
blueprints on her floor.
In this shelter she worships,
watches it
rise, iridescent with lightness
each day further above her,
bones rising, flesh

from her flesh,
its creaking breath of two by fours
awakened
by the kiss of her hammer.

National Gallery, Ottawa

In the first paintings
little yellow sunshine people play at the base
of the polite totem poles,
senses intact.
But as the years roll by
people are left behind
forgotten, for the thick wet slicks
of light and darkness.

I was happy enough.
You had become a carver
of space and colour, modelled
after the poles you loved but now
as I turn to the large wall,
suddenly this. Shocked
at the licentiousness of greens
I grow flustered, forget to look for a title.
Eros grows up my legs.
My nipples crackle
under the promise of bark.

Surely this picture should be hidden by draperies?
Emily, such a tree from you, sixty years old
and eccentric as all get out
with your monkey and dogs
promenading on Government Street.
A Victorian woman you, and yet
these paintings show no shame, as if
you wouldn't even shriek when another pole
huge, dark, male
entered your canvas, straining
to meet with the sky.

It gets worse on the next wall
and I am afraid to meet the eyes
of other tourists, afraid
they will see the lust carved here.

I fall into a chair for relief.
Give me a cool Harris, someone,
a merely obsessive Michael Snow!

Emily, you! Old and fat and dare to flaunt
such spirit! Is this why Lawren Harris
encouraged you from a distance? Surely he
licked his lips when another of those
cedar heavy boxes arrived, breathing

musk and dark while
his own canvases lay frozen in ice?

It must have been you, stroked
his Arctic blues into balance,
the passion of the perfect
Canadian businessman
for the west's romance.

British Columbia Forest

Emily, I could taste you,
the salad of your palette,
bitter chocolate of tree trunks
and totem poles climbing into skies drenched
with green and blue and light.

And down below,
when green ran like smoke through the forest,
ripe with the smell of feasts coming,
what did you do then, hungry
on your little camp stool, in your caravan,
with only the poles and the trees and the paint?

Old Tree At Dusk

A Victorian woman,
alone in a simple life
in her boarding house,
after she puts her tenants to bed

sneaks out the back door
like any teenager
into the bed of the forest
splashes through paint
to this cedar fountain
with love flowing lush
from its arms.

I love trees better than people, she says
yet this old tree leaves her mourning.
It is a love affair that cannot last.
He is taken

and she has changed
since she lifted her eyes
from his hot living trunk
to the night sprayed sky
of his arms, his eyes.

#71

She says if I lay my head against a tree
in a storm
I will hear a vibrating chord.
It is the drone of storm, she says.
The forest sings with it.

Someday I shall tell her
that the desert too, clamours and wails
a streak of shining mica.

I shall tell her the desert is a diva
laced with veins, schists
in violet, sienna and gold
under a pale ochre skin.

This is what I yearn to paint—
   She who is terrifying
   She who is buried
   She who fills your mouth with ash

wind over mesa, the song of her weeping.

#82

Fall arrives,
the season of darkness. Now at last
the tourists leave
and I am alone in the desert
where night comes early.

The air is brilliant as I perch
on a thin lip of rock.
I wear darkness, black
as a crow
        eyes bright.
Shadow is the place
that interests me.
Under these dark wings
I hide my stubborn bones.

I look for breaks in the light, bodies
of shape or colour, stone or sand —
everything is a model for my eye, my hand
the paint.

I am never tentative,
strike fast and deep.
My eyes pry open light and dark
and meaning. The rest of the time
I am silent as a bird of prey
hunting images that thrill me.

My Buddhist neighbours say,
We are love or we are fear
but I am neither, hover
in the middle, pinned tight
to my solitary nourishment.

#87

I dream a wild wind over my bare bones,
a terrifying song through the cavities of my skull,
my hips. The thin digits of what once were
articulating fingers, trail paint.

I am reduced to light   wind.
I can feel myself inside this body
like hills, like a vaulted room,
like spans or poles set
bone-deep in pearly earth.

A dark shell falls away, light rising
through translucent flesh.
I am haunted by skeletons, stripped clean
of blood and dirt.
Shaken, I vibrate to the sensations
that were once this body. The wind whistles
music through these bones.

Brenda Brooks

Brenda Brooks was born in Rivers, Manitoba. Her first book of poetry is Somebody Should Kiss You (Ragweed, 1988). She now lives and works on Salt Spring Island, and is currently at work on a novel.

January 5 p.m.

Last year my heart was a room
with a soft blaze at the centre,
or so I thought; a room without corners
for the snowy dark to settle into
in winter at five o'clock,

a room without winter,

just small, round windows bevelled
for the sun, and for the moon,
that sender of the wildest
of desired words touched with red,
streaked with gold:

pillows filled with the down
of deep blue geese (whether or not
there are such things as deep blue
geese), a bed of aromatic smoke
curling in the light, and fine
soft needles from a pine so rare
it is never found.

In truth it is several years later
and the sun has taken forever,

the moon is an echo, a cool lunar nuance
through a splintered dark

and I see snow collecting
at sharp angles in my room
at five o'clock.

My room, my heart:
how far are we now,
how far are we ever
from one torn chair
and glass underfoot,
the long traipse out the door
of tenderness and desire,

everything we knew
packed away and repossessed

except longing—

that hard, open fire
burning at the
centre.

Climax

This morning
the rain, the lover
who tips my head back
furthest, the lover
I make myself wide
for, withdrew
her fingers
from the mossy
pond and ran
her hands down
the length
of me
twice:

half my life
is over.

Losing It All

Maybe it happens like this:

One day
our smart raincoats
with toffee buttons,
our single-needle shirts
and silver tie-clips,
our silk socks and initialled scarves
draping our necks like stolen
rainbows,

one day our legitimate façades
escape us

and instead of leaving downtown
after warm croissants and chocolate,
we get stuck there, day and night,

nothing to do
but get to know the sidewalks,
the newest gaps in fences,
the best banks for heat.

On streetcars we touch ourselves
and ask intimate questions
of people we insist on knowing,
demanding they be candid,
giving everyone a touch of
claustrophobia.

On winter nights
we ride the subway
as far north as it goes
wearing socks on our hands,
then ride it back again
ignoring the ads
for cake that is faster than sex,
boxes of tissue hatching into doves,
buxom wool sweaters folding you
into their arms like a sorry mother,
loving gloves that slide their hands
into yours and softly beg you
to marry them.

We sit with the vagrant's patience
re-reading the letter we got in 1969
until a stranger too tired to know
better lets her head fall onto
our shoulder and dreams for us.

Maybe it doesn't happen exactly like this.
Maybe we keep our smart raincoats

and it happens some other way.

Moon Passes on the Right of a Broken Heart

Moon passes on the right,
nothing to do but keep driving,

scream maybe,
toss a mango out
the window at 140.

Don't slow down.
Turn here.

Glimpse yourself in the rearview
and think —
time for a haircut
when hair becomes
the sole marking for a passage
of time.

Check the truckers' cast-off butts
as they spray across the asphalt at 1 a.m.
Light one up yourself and think
firefly.

Open up
and head home on every side road
feeling like October,
feeling like everything
coming into view.

Think about stopping
at every phone booth lit up
in the dark, just to say

she was right
about the way a small, blue light
in the dash on the night's hundredth mile
pierces every place in you that ever
longed and wanted.

Don't brake.

Keep driving.
Think something easy and light and lost;
sweetness right up to your wrist.

Mango behind you,
firefly ahead.

Don't slow down.

George Elliott Clarke

George Elliott Clarke was born in Three Mile Plains, Nova Scotia, in 1960. He is the author of a poem-novel, Whylah Falls *(1990); a libretto, "Beatrice Chancy" (1998); a verse-tragedy,* Beatrice Chancy *(1999); a stage play,* Whylah Falls: The Play *(1999); a feature film screenplay,* One Heart Broken Into Song *(1999); a narrative lyric suite,* Execution Poems *(2001); and a book of poems,* Blue *(2001). His plays and opera have been produced in Halifax, Ottawa, Toronto and Edmonton. His awards and honours include the prestigious Portia White Prize (1998), a Rockefeller Foundation Bellagio (Italy) Fellowship (1998), the Toronto Black Film and Video Network's Outstanding Screenwriter Award (2000), and honorary doctorates bestowed by Dalhousie University (1999) and the University of New Brunswick (2000).* Whylah Falls *received the Archibald Lampman Award for Poetry, and* Beatrice Chancy *was shortlisted for the Atlantic Poetry Prize and the Dartmouth Book Award. George Elliott Clark teaches World Literature in English at the University of Toronto. In 2001 he was awarded the Governor General's Literary Award for Poetry.*

The River Pilgrim: A Letter

à la manière de Pound

At eighteen, I thought the Sixhiboux wept.
Five years younger, you were lush, beautiful
Mystery; your limbs—scrolls of deep water.
Before your home, lost in roses, I swooned,
Drunken in the village of Whylah Falls,
And brought you apple blossoms you refused,
Wanting Hank Snow woodsmoke blues and dried smelts,
Wanting some milljerk's dumb, unlettered love.
     That May, freights chimed xylophone tracks that rang
To Montréal. I scribbled postcard odes,
Painted *le fleuve Saint-Laurent comme la Seine*—
Sad watercolours for Negro exiles
In France, and dreamt Paris white with lepers,
Soft cripples who finger pawns under elms,
Drink blurry into young debauchery,
Their glasses clear with Cointreau, rain, and tears.
     You hung the moon backwards, crooned crooked poems
That no voice could straighten, not even O
Who stroked guitars because he was going
To die with a bullet through his stomach.

Innocent, you curled among notes—petals
That scaled glissando from windows agape,
And remained in southwest Nova Scotia,
While I drifted, sad and tired, in the east.

I have been gone four springs. This April, pale
Apple blossoms blizzard. The garden flutes
E-flats of lilacs, G-sharps of lilies.
Too many years, too many years, are past . . .

Past the broken, Cubist guitars of Arles,
Shelley, I am coming down through the narrows
Of the Sixhiboux River. I will write
Beforehand. Please, please come out to meet me
As far as Beulah Beach.

The Wisdom of Shelley

You come down, after
five winters, X,
bristlin' with roses
and words words words,
brazen as brass.
Like a late blizzard,
you bust in our door,
talkin' April and snow and rain,
litterin' the table
with poems —
as if we could trust them!

I can't.
I heard pa tell ma
how much and much he
loved loved loved her
and I saw his fist
fall so gracefully
against her cheek,
she swooned.

Roses
got thorns.
And words
do lie.

I've seen love
die.

The Symposium

Don't gimme nothin' to jaw about, Missy, and I won't have nothin' to holler for! Just sit back, relax, and be black. I'm gonna learn you 'bout the mens so you can 'scape the bitter foolishness I've suffered. A little thoughtful can save you trouble.

Missy, you gotta lie to get a good man. And after you gets him, you gotta be set to hurt him, so help my Chucky! 'Cos if you don't or won't or can't, you're gonna be stepped on, pushed 'round, walked out on, beat up on, cheated on, worked like a black fool, and cast out your own house.

Don't suck your teeth and cut your eyes at me! I be finished in a hot second. But you'll hear this gospel truth so long you, my oldest, eat and sleep in my house. Best cut your sass!

Pack a spare suitcase, one for him. If he proves a lucifer, it be easier to toss him out that way. Put one change of clothes into it so he can't beg and bug you for nothin'!

If he be too quiet, he'll ruminate and feel that bottle more than he will you. Rum'll be his milk and meat for months. It'll spoil him for anything. Won't be fit to drive his nail no mo'. So when he's sleepy drunk, smack the long-ass son of a gun in the head, tell him to wake his black-ass body up, and drive him out. If the fair fool don't come back sober, he don't come back. Am I lyin'?

And if he be sweet-lookin', a heavy-natured man, always pullin' on women, and he takes up with some spinny woman all daddlied up from the cash he's vowed to bring you, just tell him right up and down that you ain't his monkey in a dress, and raise particular devil. Don't give him no shakes. And if that don't work, don't waste another black word. Grab yourself a second man.

Watch out for two-faced chroniclers. These women will grin in your face, lookin' for news 'bout you and your man. And just when you trust their trashy talk and make your man groan and grump and get all upset, these gold-dust whores creep behind your back, crawl right in your bed, and thief him away. That's how they act. I know: I've been gypped so bloody much. And they don't care if it's a used love, a second-hand love, a stolen love, 'cos it's love all the same. And if it's good to you, they'll try to trick some too. So don't put no business on the streets that's conducted 'tween your sheets. But if some big-mouth humbugs you, tell the black bitch not to mess 'cos she's terrible lookin' anyways; a knife gash 'cross her face would just be improvement.

Missy! Gimme some of that bottle! Preachin' parches the throat. Besides, my eyes feel kinda zigzaggy today.

If some woman's grinnin' at your man, tell her straight: "If it was shit that I had, you'd want some of that too."

Make her skedaddle. If her fresh fool follows, take
Everything he got and don't give a single black penny back!

 Missy, life's nothin' but guts, muscle, nerve. All you gotta
do is stay black and die.

[*page 101*]

DEAL: I'm gonna get myself free. Get myself free. Uh huh!
In the tousled bush, I'll guttle blackberries, wild cherries,
and hazelnuts. I'll jig eel and rig me fresh eel pie. I'll gulp
dandelion coffee after dicin up the roots, roastin em in a
hardscrabble stone-oven, then stirrin the dust into boilin
water in the pot I'll liberate to cover wages owed. I'll eat
bee pollen and strawberry leaves and blueberries from
burnt-over acres. I'll mix a decoction of milk and daisies,
the meal of daylily, the morning's dew, and a smidgen of
clover. The wind'll fix my banquet. I'll slog out in the
damp, bed down in bogs, take rocks for my pillow, and
willingly suffer smelly, hot fens, mosquito swamps,
and agues and fevers. I'll venture every hidden space of
a well-hidden road. When I come out of the woods, I'll
lap rainwater from my sore palms. I expect it'll hold the
sugar taste of freedom.

Beatrice is in black in a black cell. Monday, October 5. To conceive of her inquisitors, think of swine.

BEATRICE: (*Monotone*) I pinned a viper's eye to something
      that hurt.
His blood gusted across my palm.
I stuck a coffin smack in his neck.
    Consider that I was never free,
Never safe from an invoice of shame,
My heart cracked open and there was only extinction.
    That night, fusillades of rain smashed French horns,
That night, horses whickered in the murk,
That night, five months past, I was deadly as a church,
    I'd rubbed raw the New Testament, weeping,
The Old Testament, praying. I cut him
Two gashes, and he bled like a butcher.
    White men, you took away my freedom
And gave me religion.
So be it: I became a devout killer.

BEATRICE: Maybe you forgets, Deal, how we once dashed,
    Crashing night-long beneath moth-pestered lamps,
    Laughter splashing hot like rum in our throats,
    Moonlight joshing gilt, delirious hay —
    How we turned and turned, heathenish in grass,
    And Lead joked I had a face like a horse,
    Then drawled that I was woeful beautiful,
    And we uprooted brash buttercups to suck,
    And Dice whined and whined for our strawberries,
    And we'd never give him a single taste.

CHANCY: Taste Grand Pré wine,
  Annapolis sharp cheese,
  Windsor salt butter,
  Madeira Portuguese;
  Jamaican dark rum,
  Adam's rain-pale ale,
  Pickled melon, chicken,
  Cornbread, spiced pigtails;
  Oysters, fried scallops,
  Gaspereaux, and clams,
  Queen Eliza cake,
  Apples, sides-a-ham;
  Sour coffee, sweet cream,
  And chokecherry pie.
  A wicked kick of whisky,
  Newfie screech, or rye.

Elegy for Mona States (1958–1999)

I

At nine, we tussled and frolicked, golden, in hayfields,
Your yellow hair inflamed and nerve-wracking as sunlight,
While elders tucked a ceased, earthen father into earth,
And your laughter resembled sugar sparkling in tea.
No, your voice was like a silk scarf holding gravel —
Or like the rasp of water over bristling stone,
During that wake, after that awakening,
When September shook gold on your face and hair,
Cousin, and I imagined more than nine-year-olds should,
For you were a gangling, loud, anarchic song,
All the music in you crying through your skin,
And your lips on a *Mr. Frostee* root beer
Were a singer's lips caressing a poem.
    At eleven, we worshipped *Diamonds Are Forever*,
The penultimate Connery-incarnated Bond,
And your wheat hair so outshone the cinematic light,
I was sure you'd go to sumptuous Hollywood,
To Hollywood, and shimmer election down on us
From some expansive, tremendous screen,

Some veil of honeyed luminescence,
Because, Mona, your name conjured up Desdemona—
Othello's ivory-silvery bride—Ramona,
That heroine of a thousand Nashville folk tunes,
And because your name had a peculiar, rural allure,
Suggesting to preachers a new-style Norma Jean,
And because a moaning smoke tang singed your gold hair,
And some arch, beautiful wound scarred your green eyes.

After watching the original *The Secret Garden*,
We went careening in dangerous glee—
Down a marvelously tumbling, green-black hill,
Crowded with pale shrubs and gooey, spectacular ectoplasm,
Down to the knife-edge of glinting, licorice-coloured water,
In Dartmouth, where my folks were coming apart
Like an obsolete car engine,
But we dreamed and wept for a life as in the movies,
Where you would be *Perfection*
And poets would lavish you homage in hit-parade poems.

Instead, you acted sex spoofs in a one-bedroom hut,
With Absalom (not his real name), all grizzle and gristle,
Who liked to fondle you in dirty, exciting secrecy
Under the welfare-cheque-thin covers,
Before committing criminally stupid infractions
So that he could go blithely to Springhill Penitentiary,
To try penance for his intoxicated thieving
And foul-mouthed, foul-breathed, sucker punches,

And wash his smashed face and clip his yucky sideburns.
Waiting, you played a delicious wraith, homely, winsome—
Like The Hollies' *Long Cool Woman in a Black Dress*—
Une belle rebelle toasted with Coca-Cola and rum.

You flowered from thirteen to twenty—
Your astonishing years of dreams,
Letting your voice ebb all cigarettish, wispy with tarnation,
And wearing some deep black dress to offset such sun-fired hair
And exhibit a supremely seditious sinuosity.
You learned how to break down engines into parts
And to chitchat about loathsome, too-real, splatter films,
So that our Secret Garden became long-gone ruins,
Your airy, Fabergé looks withered like worn-out Levi's,
And your bards devolved into hirsute, auto body creeps
Burbling in their suds for their mothers and fave pin-ups.
You became a knife that filletted the fog of Friday night
Dance floors, tavern fisticuffs, and suicidal hangovers,
So that the drunks' alternative wives worried
Your too-frank beauty would sack their husbands.

Once, in those years, I learned the word *aphasia*,
While sitting crooked and alcohol-wrecked at your table,
September twilight enlightening the thesaurus (*Roget's*),
And hickory smoke bittersweetening your lemony hair,
And you babied me with *Kahlua* and vodka,
Something like Hitchcock's *Topaz* dazzling the TV,

Because another blonde gal had havocked my heart,
And you pitied me, becoming, again for me,
Jock Sturges' Mona or Liz Montgomery of *Bewitched*,
Not a stylishly ragged magdalen of bootleg and smack,
Shacked up with a disgusting, urine-dull idol—
His felon's grungy, infinitesimal brain—
And your car coming apart like parents in divorce court.

       Years afterward, you still rambled bouldered trails,
Then volcanic ruins of genealogy and lust,
Playing an explorer who could only find horror—
The tombstone of your rotted, demobbed-drunkard dad—
Though you did spin two daughters off Spanish Andy,
A one-time husband, and you posted me cards
And photos of your fitfully happy motherhood and marriage,
But, even here, the solitude of alcohol intruded,
And your gambled family vanished into the courts,
And you traipsed in and out of the mental institution,
Until you took a chair and sat down outside your trailer,
Somewhere on Panuke Road, in Three Mile Plains,
Where we had guffawed in the hayfield—
O my darling, darling, darling Mona—
And you gazed at pictures of your blonde daughters,
And cocked a gun and stuck it at your forehead
And abolished yourself—
Drowning impeccable gold light under crude black earth.

We moaned in the wheatfield like poets in their
               youth—
Finding a system of wonder and waste,
Amid crickets and torn-off buttons and our smells of milk,
A copy of *Romeo and Juliet* bulging from a pocket,
Or we spoke hoarse, in horse-play, with things in a basket,
And I said you had a face exactly like a horse—
The phrase *palomino blonde* was black liquor in my brain—
But your skinny, thrilling, Kodak beauty set me hoarse.
The jack-o-lantern-orange moon that unscrolled over us
Promised strange, malevolent miracles of union,
And I desired you in breathy leather or gossamer calico,
Something countryish and vaguely exotic,
And I yearned to watch you lick and swallow raspberries,
Your *Mona Lisa* smile being richly no forgery,
In a night falling coal and dewy and green with weeds,
So we'd get wet and grass stains on our clothes
Where we'd fall, night mauving our faces with dew,
And entertain a moist wedding of lips—
Forgetting principalities of arrest and alarm,
And I dreamt of your skin, its softness like far stars.
But we were cousins, first-cousins, first of all,
So there was no appeal to sex appeal,
Only apple peels, or the peal of the Baptist church bells,

Dragging Uncle Charlie from his tinderbox guitar,
His smile like kindling, his slippered feet shuffling
Fluidly and sweetly as Red Rose tea or Don Messer violin
   or rumour
Or soured card games scattered upon sour linoleum,
His voice elongating Three Mile Plains into the Sahara,
Scorpions riding every blistering guitar string.
Sublimated, we kicked pebbles and gulped pound cake
And Alexander Keith's India Pale Ale,
Remonstrated about car engines, their discomfiture,
And remembered that we was niggerish injuns,
Half-Black Mi'kmaqs, our times full of broken cylinders,
Cocky, no-bullshit, bill collectors, battery casings shot,
Miserable, last shots at love, and shot-down lovers.
Our schools opened up truancy and failure before us;
Our lovers were skittish and fickle as minnows.
I chased after a blonde or two: they were cool tadpoles;
You got a babbling, yahoo-hoodlum of a blonde.
Then, you wed a dark-haired man and got two blonde girls.
But you never had peace with anyone who understood
The splendour of Green Tomato Chow-Chow in the morning
Or the paradise of milk and molasses at night,
Or whose laughter licked black against a bleak harbour,
Or who laid out crispy, spiced chicken on a bleached pine table,
Or who talked to you in amiable, sermonic tones.
So you have broken your face with a bullet,

Smithereened your own da Vincian portrait,
But I carry, still, your shimmering face—
The image of Ophelia's black water-bordered face—
In my head: it shines through smoke and mirages.
But there will never be the photographs that could have been,
Only this poem closing its gilt sarcophagus upon you.

Jealousy

à la manière de Saavedra

I could pummel the wind
for daring to splay
your silver, virgin hair.

I could blind the sun
for eyeing you so hotly,
so possessively.

I could batter the rain
for so libertinely
moistening your gold face.

I could stab the vulgar air
for always stepping
so bodily between us.

I could behead the roses
for snatching their scent
from you as you pass.

I could burn the grass
that dews your brown feet
without my permission.

And those ivory sheets
that clasp you all night?
Why, I could strangle them!

Glen Downie

Formerly a social worker in cancer care, Glen Downie *currently serves as Writer-in-Electronic-Residence to the Medical Humanities Program of Dalhousie University's Faculty of Medicine. He has published four books of poetry, read his work across Canada and in the US, and appeared in several anthologies and dozens of literary journals. In addition to poetry, he has published fiction, non-fiction, translations, film and book reviews and co-edited the work-writing anthology* More Than Our Jobs. *His latest book is* Wishbone Dance (*Wolsack & Wynn, 1999*).

The Deceased   POST-MORTEM REPORT

She had cancer
then a stroke
left her thoughts wired wrong
She used a child's Magic Slate
when she couldn't find words

I'm too young to be so sick she said
then she wrote on the slate: 34
When the sheet was pulled up
her age disappeared
like magic

Dominion

We flatter ourselves
that some of them actually like us—
dogs, because they can be made to serve,
and dolphins, because they are always smiling

There are others we cannot fathom, willful creatures
who have chosen ugly bodies, impenetrable speech
They feel no guilt, have found no reason
to envy us   We keep them penned
in rows, like enemy prisoners
        There is a bird from some place in South
        America that rips out the kidneys
        of sheep with its hooked beak
        To stand by its cage is to be measured
        In a dark mirror   The bird claws at the dirt
        Its wicked mouth scissoring air

We long ago wearied of naming them   We keep them now
Out of frustration, out of fear   If we dared
We might kill them.

Jim Green

Jim   Green   was born and raised in southwestern Alberta. Green has lived and worked throughout the north in Lac la Martre, Spence Bay on the Arctic Coast, Yellowknife and Fort Smith on the Slave River, where he lives now. Jim is a widely published poet, author and raconteur whose work includes Beyond Here *(Thistledown, 1983), a collection of poetry; and* Flint & Steel, *an album with musician Pat Buckna.*

from NORTH BOOK (1986)

Every Day

Every day
for damn near two months
she scraped seal skins
bent over   head down
with stomach cramps
and letting 'lots of air'
from the rich meat

But by God
she kept at it
scraped green hides
pegged them down
rolled them   aired them
til she had sixteen
and they broke camp
headed for town
with enough to trade
for a washing machine

Netsiksiuvik

The Fish Eye Poem

my prize char
stiff   on the ice
a sleek dark beauty
my first char
with a spear

lifting my head
from the dark ice hole
I turn around
and there's a kid
with a knife in hand
bent over my fish

he pries with the blade
an eye pops out
down dives his head
teeth snatch it
he jumps up
walks away chewing

and there it is
my prize char
laid out on the ice
staring at me
blankly
eye socket
vacant

Lord Lindsey Lake

Half Dance

for Takolik

A hundred parka clad folks
a lot of them little kids
in a 20 × 30 foot Quanset hut
where the record player's jumping
booted feet stomping
arms swinging
faces laughing
and it's
   Dance Night
in the ol' home town.
People jammed along the walls
on sagging plywood benches
legs bouncing
toes tapping
kids are falling on the floor.
Babies wide eyed
peer from mothers' backs
pop cans clatter
kicked across the room
by screaming boys
and in the middle of it all
   the dancers.
Takolik calling out the moves

picked up from older times
in over two hundred years
of concertinas whalers
and whatnot
down through time
to the cook shack
on Friday night.
Doe si doe
and a-la-man left
don't know the words
but it's what we do
arms across
star center
swing your partner
it gets faster
you lose all track
go charging right along
following the half dance
half round
half square
half the night
you keep going on and on
cowboy boots stamping
seal skin boots thumping
babies bouncing
hands squeezing

then all join hands
rush to the center
back up to the walls
again to the center
all hands in the air
for a final shout . . .

      it's over.

Steam clouds roll in
from the opened door
fifty cigarettes are lit
and they're lining up
around the tea kettle
knees quivering
smiling.

    Spence Bay

    jan.25.74

Angela Hryniuk

Angela Hryniuk has been a street worker, foster parent, musician's manager, publishers' rep and book-keeper, and now makes her living as a writer, editor and freelance publicist.

Her first book, walking inside circles, was published by gynergy books in 1989. Her Polestar book, no visual scars, was released in 1993.

from NO VISUAL SCARS (1993)

entwined

hazy light dim in London
I've just finished a glass of brandy
you are in the bath reading
my mother next door feels sorry for herself
wants to return to Canada probably cried herself to sleep
I step into your room double bed on the floor
covers folded back. I see a tiny blue flame
flicker hear a soft hiss from the gas fire
I undress jump into bed light still on
as you enter the room close the door
remove your long white terrycloth housecoat
& crawl in beside me. you shut the light
wind the clock in darkness & reach over
curl around me. a seahorse. soft body
nudges into mine. I have never felt the erect nipples
of another woman's breasts on my back
before. your hands dance on the front of my body
my breasts. my sides. down my thighs. you
wrap your finger loosely around the curls
of my hair. I turn & face you kiss
my forehead. I pull my knees to my chest you

wrap your legs around my body cradle me
as though I've taken a bad fall.
our bodies twist & tangle.
as you undress tonight I thought
what a beautiful pear-shaped body you have. yes
I remember you.
when I phoned & asked
how would we recognize each other
at the airport
you laughed.

from **between two oceans**

I find remnants of you
lying around people's houses
I walk into Linda's
see a guitar
propped against the wallpapered wall
assume it's yours

I visit Michael
have a coffee & chat
out of the corner of my eye I see
a box of your clothes

slowly I walk home
along the water's edge
want something tangible
to remember you by
as I enter the bedroom
I notice on the floor
an ashtray with a butt
from your lips squished
by your thumb
buried in ashes
beside the bed
the blue '67 Valiant crosses my path

many times each day
I walk across Baker Street
see your car & look for your face
your body hunched over the wheel
but know we're between two oceans

weeks pass
even months
& still
you're here
in my red heart
keeps moving
city after city
you too
never stand still
to stagnate to stammer to
stutter or shuffle no
always in motion
by plane by bike by foot by
& bye

don't want him to kiss me
his lips are soft
his brown skin is smooth
don't want to twist to face him
his body is strong & gentle
the insides of my body turn
slowly so do I
still my lips touch
our eyes
in darkness
bodies beneath the sheets
I turn away
think of you
elsewhere

Aislinn Hunter

Aislinn Hunter was born in Belleville, Ontario and moved to Dublin, Ireland for a few years before making her home in British Columbia. She received a BFA from the University of Victoria and an MFA from the University of British Columbia. She has published her poetry widely in literary journals in Canada and abroad, and is also the author of a much-praised book of fiction, What's Left Us *(Polestar, 2001). Into the Early Hours is her first book of poetry. She lives in Vancouver, British Columbia with her husband and their dog Fiddler.*

Raising A Glass In A Field Near Galway

Back into the march grass and mud, the four of us go,
pint glasses in hand, searching for the one glass gone missing,
the one nursed like a child these two miles from Spiddal,
conveyed over rutted roads and trenches
past the "do not enter" plaque at the edge of the field,
though we trudged on anyway, like swimmers in the long grass,
folded into the accordion of its limbs.

Nearby sheep settle into the warmth of their fleece,
and the bull we reeled by eyes us
from behind the barbed wire of his fence.
Sudden grace, or lack thereof, that we found the glass
after ten minutes, the three of you having gone down
on hands and knees, genuflecting in the direction of the town.

But what does it matter? Hourglass or bathysphere,
telescope or jar, we raise it to the night's throat,
we drink the morning. Treble of bullrush and moor-grass
on our tongues, we carry on walking.
Cut through the field like one body, content to tread until dawn.

Recollection

The slim-wristed dead are with you again,
in their ruffled blouses and long white skirts —
two young girls, feet slung out of the hammock
on Chatham street, sleeping and as still as fish
too long out of water, mouths open
under a bright canopy of sun. It's late summer
and every afternoon has been like this one

but for your hand on the banister of the back porch,
as incongruous as an airplane in an apple grove.
That you can touch her shoulder and wake her,
along with her sister and the small brown terrier
curled up in the shade. That the oak tree's leaves
feather your neck as you stand beside them.

She wakes up slowly and enters the house,
as if it still existed, and the two of them
climb kitchen chairs and pick through the pantry
for snacks. Spread jam on bread then dip their fingers
in the jar. How young they are now,
and how forgotten. Her memories at work in you,
smell of the countryside when you wake.

Climbing Lessons

Hand over hand I climbed the ladder of my grandfather's body,
the leg braces under his brown trousers like steps
to a tree house, the only way up — the arch of my bare foot
finding the metal circle around his ankle, my toes curling over it,
that thin band as familiar as a favourite pair of shoes.

Then my left knee making for his lap, for the top of his leg brace,
leverage to haul myself up, like our dog's collar
one summer when she pulled me, holding on, up a hill.
There was never any turning back, no hoisting by the arms.
In my grandfather's house you did things of your own volition.

His hand a compass, how he would tap his chest, say 'come here'
as I crawled over mountains to see him, to stretch out
in the hammock of his arms, bury my head between shirt and
        cardigan.
The thrum of his heart in my ear, intake of breath like wind
at the tent flaps. And I waited there, eyes closed,

made mental lists of the provisions I would need to get home.
The cuff of his sweater a handhold, the pleats of his pants
        a kind of rope.

It was up there I said my prayers before sleeping, never sure
of where we were as he walked around the house. That
        darkness
like a country I wanted to enter.

Sometimes the rain came like hands tapping on the roof, then
the trickling stream of runoff from the gutters, all the
        sounds of the house
wrapped around us like a blanket. While outside the porch light
shone like a sun busy in other hemispheres. My grandfather
        moving
into the place beyond it, long after I'd climbed down.

Scorsese's Last Temptation of Christ

It must be transfiguration, that dream
where Willem Dafoe is with me
under a mound of blankets,
curled up on the wrong side of my bed.

My knees nudged into the backs of his,
my breasts nestled between his shoulder blades,
and I'm wearing my best pair of flannel pajamas—
the blue ones, white pinstripes.

And suddenly it occurs to me, my hands
palm down against the flat of his chest—
I'm spooning Christ,
so I inch my fingers along, over his ribcage.

They don't hang you on the cross with ribbons,
he tells me, that being the reason why
his hands and feet get so cold,
why he bundles the blankets around them

why he always sleeps on the same side.
Then he turns, opens his arms for me, Willem Dafoe,
and I go in to the smell of sleep, stale gin
the cigarettes he smoked the night before,

then I turn my back to him, my bum wiggling
into his groin until we are joined perfectly,
until his hands find mine, and he anoints them
with his lips, one finger at a time.

Walking the Dog

A short-cut through the city, past pot-holes,
the sloped roofs of carports, and now and again,
the outstretched arms of fern
appearing between garbage bins.
I know this hour of the day,
who will be home, what lights will be on,
how the black Jetta will reverse into the garage
at five-forty p.m.
These alleyways, the back doors of people's lives,
unswept and cluttered, the grass growing over
the edge of the patio, the cat passing hours
pressing her cheek against glass.

The dog trots ahead of me, and the noise of traffic
swells around us, rush hour heading down roads
on the far side of these houses.
I hear tin cans clattering into the recycle,
a window sliding into its latch.
The mongrel down the block bays again
and above us power lines hum, split the sky
into horizons, a series of wide screens
the birds wing across before cutting out
in the opposite direction.

Almost winter and these walks are shorter,
the alleys settling into evening like failing lungs,
and even the dog ready to turn home after half an hour,
the raccoons getting ready to make their rounds
as I button my coat up to the chin.
Past us another light flicks on in someone's kitchen,
all of us heading into our own distant lives,
or turning to go home.

This is philosophy, dusk descending like a curtain,
the leaves that mark the lateness of the season
browning in the absence of light,
raked into seams along the edge of the yard.
Here, a row of tomatoes leans into frost
like blood pearls on the vine
and walking the dog I believe the city into being
even though there is only
the fall of light from a bedroom window,
a metal shed, the sound of pots in a kitchen,
to convince me.
The alleyway sloped as we walk along it,
and in parts, lilting.

Paulette Jiles

Paulette Jiles's poetry collection Celestial Navigation
*(McClelland and Stewart, 1984) won the Pat Lowther Memorial
Award, the Gerald Lampert Award and the Governor General's
Award — the first time one book has won all three awards. She is
also the author of* Waterloo Express *(poetry) and two books of
fiction,* Sitting in the Club Car Drinking Rum & Karma-Kola
(Polestar) and The Late Great Human Road Show *(Talon).
Paulette Jiles' novel,* Enemy Women, *will be released by
HarperCollins Canada in February 2002.*

Jesse Meets His Future Wife, Zee Mimms

Here she is coming in with medicines, with bandages for
his infected life.
She can see everything in this big hole in his thoughts.
She can see the faulty reason beating and beating,
the lost causes,
the parts that are missing, the blood and the lungs.

There are things that live inside of wounds;
a certain memory fixed in his body forever,
a hole in the heart of Dixie, just south of his breastbone.
It was the last time he ever exposed his heart.
It was the last time he ever put his hands
above his head
except for her.

Every man is owed a wife; wives live in a different
          country,
a country of women without civil wars, or trains, or
          motivations.

They arrive with bandages; he imagines they never
        surrender
except to him.

She will make a design of his life, a quilt pattern
rusty with blood, made up of the rags
of women's dresses.
Log Cabin, Courthouse Steps, The Road to
        California.

He says: Marry me.
He says: I want to be able to stop,
just stop and watch you,
a hawk pouring out of the long prairie air
carrying between your wings a commission from the
        fertile sun
and your soul, which will have to serve for us both
and move through us both
like a wind through the bottom fields
an invisible comb, I will be moved and marked
and finally harvested.
Why don't you marry me, he says. Tend to all these
wars, and the broken thoughts, and the open wounds.

Frank Retires

I'll shake hands with anybody that
walks up the road.
At the age of forty-nine almost anybody who matters
to me is dead,
in the simple and uneventful woods
most by violence.

When I handed in my guns, everything stopped.
It stopped, and there was no more screaming,
the sound of running horses and black powder,
it was all gone.

How slowly people move
and with what patience the horses search
for horseweed in the fields.
I am amazed, I am amazed with what fixed intent
we move from the porch into supper.
I sit down carefully, I am astonished at everything—
the plates with flowers, my big old mother praying
over the food and my shiny hands.
I am free as the unemployed goldenrod and the
        clouds
move in from Kansas, dry and clean.

Raising Hogs

September of 1876 Frank rides quietly away from
        Northfield
toward Tennessee like the whole thing was just
        embarrassing;
it was hardly human, he won't let Jesse drag him into
these things again.
Frank's going to Tennessee and raise hogs
he crosses the river at Cape Girardeau
it's a very hot river town, the Mississippi is actually
        hot
it's steaming, nobody asks who you are.
He is seduced by all the simple normal people at the
ferry landing, he will send for Annie and the kids,
he is crossing the river into Little Egypt
he's going into agriculture as if it were a religion
the Holy Fire Church of Prophesy and Pigs.
There will be peace in Waverly County
they have relatives down there they can count on
never go anyplace you don't have relatives.
It's all in how a man comports himself
walking upright amongst the swine.

Joy Kogawa

Joy Kogawa was born in Vancouver, British Columbia. She achieved international prominence with the publication of her novel Obasan *(Penguin), which dealt with the experience of Japanese-Canadians during World War II. For this work, she received numerous awards, including the American Book Award. Kogawa has also published several books of poetry, fiction for young people, and the novels* Itsuka *and* The Rain Ascends. *Joy Kogawa is a recipient of the Order of Canada. She lives in Toronto, Ontario, where she writes and is active in community work.*

And in the hour of Eve asleep
Mammon the Almighty Consumer
Rumbles forth to ravage the earth,
Jaws yawning. It launches its feast
By nibbling eyes and all things small
All things bright and beautiful
Butterflies, tadpoles, songbirds
The flutterers, the sliders
The crawlers, the walkers
The babies in the third world
The grannies in the cold world
The sitters on street corners
The Mom and Pop shops
All, all are devoured
In Mammon's great feast.
And Mammon's corporate marketeers,
The gaunt and hollowed hunger-makers
"Whose god is their belly,"
Leap like plagues of locusts
Hobbling the inhabitants of earth.
Each in their turn become creatures
Who dance without feet
In the frenzy and heat of consumption

As they chant their creed in unison,
"Money, Money is Everything,
Money is God,"
And all earth bows down to worship It,
For the power of Love lies broken
In the dust
Howl howl,
Sweet daughters of Eve —
Howl for the sons
Mangled in the machinations of war;
Howl for the mothers, the babies
In the midst of famine
Languishing while the ones
They love more than life
Lie dying in the drought;
Cry for the daughters of Lilith
The countless strong women of the ages
Feared for their power
Condemned for their passion
Uprooted from their potential and relegated
To the empty pages of their unlived lives;
Weep for old men, old women,
Adrift on the streets
In rags against the moon,

The crones, the hags on broomsticks
Sailing the long long night
Flying in futility
The children lost

For these are the days
Of the demons at play
Roaring across the skies
Over the plains and the hills
Gleeing in their unbridled greed
While they pillage the planet
How pitiable the people of earth:
Eve against Lilith
Man against man
And Adam listless, Adam wild
Pining still
For his first love lost

Lost as well
Are the minions of Mammon —
Hearts turned to ash
Blood turned to rust.
Almighty man
Lies chastened at last
With only his rib

As soul-mate and comfort,
Only his echo
In her hand-me-down skin.
How infinitely lone,
Adam and Eve,
These lopsided lovers

Pat Lowther

Pat Lowther was one of the most original and accomplished voices in Canada's literary scene in the 1960s and early 1970s. In 1975, Pat Lowther died tragically; her husband was convicted of her murder. At the time, Lowther was poised to achieve fame as a poet. Her work was becoming widely published, she had been elected co-chair of the League of Canadian Poets and she was teaching Creative Writing at the University of British Columbia. Her death left the Canadian cultural scene mourning. She had published three collections of poetry in her lifetime; two more were published posthumously. Time Capsule (*Polestar, 1996*) collects the best work from these five books and also features new poems from an unpublished manuscript discovered by Pat Lowther's daughter more than twenty years after her death.

Riding Past

Long street of houses
with lighted roofs
black against

winter sky blue as Venetian glass
with Venus hanging
like a small yellow moon

In the houses people
are cooking food and scolding children
The ones home from work

are hanging their coats up
telephones are ringing
behind the yellow windows

Come, open the doors
yellow rectangles and steam
of meat and potatoes

Stand on the front steps
Stare at the sky and wave
Look, we're riding past Venus

Before The Wreckers Come

Before the wreckers come,
Uproot the lily
From the hard angle of earth
By the house.
Crouch by the latticed understairs
Rubbish and neglect
(The sudden lightning
Of sun
On your back
Between the opening
And shutting
Of the March-blown clothesline,
Rise and fall of the swift light
Like blows.)
Here a lifetime's
Slimy soapsuds
Curdle the earth,
In this corner
Under the stairs,
But have not killed
The woodbugs
Nor the moths' pupae
Which brush your fingers
As you dig

For the round, rich root
The lily root
Which has somehow, senselessly,
Not been killed either
But has grown every year
An astonished babyhood,
An eye-struck Easter.
Pack it among the photographs,
The silver polish,
And the last laundry
Which will not again
Lift and shutter
For the shattering sun.
Mark its container : X
Two intersecting lines,
A lattice point
Of time
And the years' seasons.

Before the wreckers come,
Carry away
The lightning-bulb of sun.

Imagine Their Generations

Imagine their generations a vertical frieze
the shapes repetitive as an ocean
the dumb curve of shoulders
bent to their work, their earth.
Each figure has one hand cupped
an ambiguous gesture, giving or holding
corn, metal, pollen, or something intricate
and bruisable as a lung; or a coal,
its fragile petals of ash protecting the hand
from the orange-pink heat
at the heart of it.

Feel their shapes in your mind
the smooth humps of shoulders
the angular jack-knife arms
the hands contracted to a calyx
Imagine now time itself grown dense
as coal, impacted
in that one posture.

John MacKenzie

John MacKenzie was born on Prince Edward Island in 1968, "one of nine children of a former schoolteacher, and a reformed-alcoholic ex-sailor turned vacuum-cleaner salesman and tent preacher." He quit school in grade seven. At thirteen, he was in reform school. At nineteen, he began to write poetry and travel across Canada. He has worked in sawmills, bakeries and kitchens, and on farms and construction crews. He lives in Charlottetown, PEI, where he is on the editorial board of blue SHIFT: A Journal of Poetry. Sledgehammer *is his first book. It was shortlisted for the Atlantic Poetry Prize and the Gerald Lampert Award for the Best First Book of Poetry.*

My love is strung with the ancient

How do I love thee   thou inward old
son of a bitch   thou self-dried
self-jailed walking gray wall of prison
guntowers & rusted barbwire   thou

inadvertent passer of genes who
gave me this face   this one short leg   this
cowboy walk?   didst the half of me burn as
it passed through thy cock?   didst thou

weaken in the knees?   did the thread of
blood between us vibrate with
these days when I walk by thee   past thee
through thee as if I don't know how

thee hates thine own face   as if
I don't know how an electric razor lets
thee shave by feel & I must ask: Is it true
vampires cannot manipulate mirrors?

I love thee with the rage of the setting
sun in my bones   in the marrow of them   in
their latticed design   in my larynx   in
the timbre of my

hello to everyone but thee   (these
I acknowledge love thee   but this body
was one of nine accidents)   I love
thee with all the scars of acne   the blackheads—

submerged poison in my flesh   I love thee with
the rage of the setting sun   with
the temperature of cigarette coals   My
love is strung with the ancient

sinews of tyrannosaurs   their extravagantly
muscled hips & perpetual coil-spring
hind-legs   their heads of mostly jaws &
teeth   I love you with all

the destruction of hydrogen bombs   the
crushing of metal against guardrails   the
ice that creeps into cells & ruptures as
it thaws

Lower the Boom

for Ivan Arsenault, killed in August 1998
on this framework of steel and rivets, this
erector set pushing into the sky

He stood here before the glass went on, stood
in and on the growing skeleton, grasping
I-beams in the heat of Ontario's August days
palms sweating in leather gloves guiding
I-beams to their appointed places, or else

he tied re-bar with those gloved hands, tied
arcane knots around slender rods
to be hidden in concrete, to hold
the whole damn thing together

This is some of what he did: woke every morning
at 4:30, ate cereal from boxes, drank
tea that steeped while he brushed teeth and shaved
threw his lunch box in the passenger's seat
tightened his boot laces and his belt
mumbled morning talk with the others
in his Miscouche accent while settling
his hardhat on dark hair, thinking maybe
about a daughter starting school soon

maybe about the Jays' game, or
more likely, being from Miscouche, wondering if
the Habs will ever find another goaltender like Dryden or Roy

This is what he did that day: woke at 4:30
ate his cereal, drank his tea
tightened his boot laces and belt and climbed
the naked steel under the climbing sun, all day
he clambered in the ring and clamour
welding this, riveting that, guiding
crane-swung bundles of steel to rest, and

most of the day he breathed
and worked, glowing like a beacon of sweat

and he argued about overtime and cursed bosses (whose
wreath—and the note saying they thought they should send it
—was thrown on the funeral-home lawn)

Yeah, he worked and cursed the bosses' bidding
on jobs they couldn't start on time and rushed
to finish on schedule, under budget
he cursed old equipment and mistakes driven by hurry
and the sloppy minds of others but . . .

the beat of hammers and the view, the
pure music of storey rising on storey, of
seeing the metal become

he could hear, some days, the steel breathe
see it pulse and grow like
the child he felt move each morning under
his callused hand on Ruth's belly

He saw the sunset as he thumbed down another bundle
he saw the sunset and, at first, when the steel slammed into him
he thought it was beauty flattening him, he believed
the glorious shattered red and purple had
fallen from the sky into him and
he remembered his Catholic upbringing
and, suddenly, the meaning of epiphany but

the others saw the scattered red as blood, the paramedics saw
the darkening glorious purple bruise he had become
and the doctor stripped off latex gloves, moved on   Ruth

miscarried

A List (By Colour) of Things Left Behind

A singular perception of green

White gusts of laughter, like this wind
Full of petals

A string of perfect, round moments
Ground to powder

One pair of boots, black and scuffed;
The rundown clocks of their heels

One blue sky, slightly used

Too many words (also down-at-the-heel)
From faces down at the mouth

My son's eyes
(But not his first, slow blink)

O We Burnt Out Our Clutches
(Riding Them Buggies of Need)

I pursued you until you became
The pursuer;
Ran me down bright streets blossomed with prostitutes of
     the word

Between the bones of factories
Where all the jammed and cross-purposed machinery of
     love rusted.
Thought was a switch frozen between the grotesque and
     the sacred,
Between gap and closure.

(Now this mouth has bid farewell to words —
These eyes have seen too many vowels spread into stained,
     white wings.
And there remains no way to tell you.)

O we clutched our secrets as we clutched one another
Till we slipped through each other's clutches —
O we burnt out our clutches.
And we shattered the gears of our love.

Nadine McInnis

Nadine McInnis's stories have been published in
The Malahat, Canadian Forum, Quarry, Event, The New
Quarterly, Canadian Fiction, Dandelion *and* Grain. *Her work
has been anthologized in* Entering the Landscape: A Room at
the Centre of Things, Quintet, Coming Attractions 1997,
Vital Signs *and* Carrying Fire. *Selections from her poetry in*
Hand to Hand *won the 1992 National Poetry Contest and took
second prize in the* CBC *Literary Competition. She was also
nominated for the Pat Lowther Award. Her two other poetry titles
include* Shaking the Dreamland Tree *and* The Litmus Body,
which won the Ottawa Carleton Book Award.

*McInnis graduated from the University of Ottawa and has
taught both there and at the University of New Brunswick.*
Quicksilver, *a collection of short stories, was published by
Raincoast Books in October 2001.*

Insomnia

I rise to swim through the night,
each foot searching for the dark stair going down
the way you sound
the depth of a rushing stream with your boot.
Will I stumble
down, not into my own living room
but into the dark pool, its darting lights
flicking across my vision
where sleep rises from silt and dissolves time.
Fish streaming above the dream of their own fossils
shiver by and I'm lost
a voice cold on my thigh, then gone,
a hand opens and gives up its heat.
I know a woman who rose each night
to the cry of a baby lost deep in a well,
stumbling blind into rooms where her children
curled with their thumbs snug as small pearls
in the closed shells of their mouths.
If I didn't go mad then, I never will,
she said years after she'd relearned
the languid sidestroke of sleep.

Walking on Water

We walked on water
to the lighthouse anchored in the channel
past Duck Island, that thin strip of trees,
unpopulated. Only the illusion of land,
a web of tree-roots snaking down
into the dingy river that moved on endlessly
while we tossed in our sleep.

We never set foot there in summer.
Only in winter were we drawn out onto the ice
where a distant blue light swung and blinded
like a migraine, like our intense longing
to move on. Hazy with desire,
that cloud of fish-flies disorienting us,
as we trudged along shore, then inched out
onto the creaky ice towards the lighthouse
where you carved my name.

Spring nights we lay
together in your parents' basement,
the river rising in the dark, voluptuous
lapping that washed our dull neighbourhood
of its omissions, train whistles far off
hurting us less in that moment,

the moan of massive shadows, imagined
as ships that moved along the river only at night,
ships we would board separately
as stowaways. You first, then me.
I looked forward to not knowing one day
where you might be.

Today I walk the shore with my children
calling them back from the allure
of the edge. For now, casting stones
is enough. They haven't looked out to where
only the concrete base of the lighthouse remains.
My name is gone. That little permanence
we risked our lives for,
swept into a black current.

A miracle, this growing up, knowing now
what the danger is called: *candle ice*,
walking on *candle ice*, pale columns
cold as wax, tunnels we might have slipped down,
flaming only with one moment's
wish, to disappear
without leaving a trace.

lunar eclipse over the Mer Bleue Bog

in the beginning there is the shape
of a breast   dusky   blood-red
pulsing with warmth in a sky
flat and deceptive as black ice

we're edgy with cold
hug ourselves and don't look down
to tiny orchids and jack-in-the-pulpits
freeze-dried into grizzled shells

the dead have withdrawn
their bones fur and fibre
plush surge of centuries   peat
that held us up soft as a lap
we kneaded with our feet is harsh

and lunar

but the moon
swung far out over the bog is flesh now
dropping heavy with its low nipple of light
swelling full

we open our mouths   chins tilted up
and light
runs down our throats
how long we've waited for this!

light eases up to the rim
an irresistible flood
lifting Canada geese shouting
from the dark channel
of open water beyond the rushes

lifting these shadows floating up
from our feet
from the trunks of trees ringing the bog
and every blade
of ambitious life lost over winter

we walk in moonlight again   above us a cup
almost full
a blazing shell open and yielding
our shadows
move and merge and part like a school of fish

netted by these flickerings   held here
by tough filaments of shadow but light
slips through

satiated   our faces are milky with it.

Shani Mootoo

Shani Mootoo was born in Ireland and grew up in Trinidad. She is the author of a book of short stories, Out on Main Street (*Press Gang*), and a novel, Cereus Blooms at Night (*McClelland and Stewart*), which was shortlisted for the Chapters First Novel Award and the Giller Prize. Her poetry has been anthologized widely. In addition to being a writer, Shani is a video-maker and visual artist whose paintings and photo-based work are exhibited internationally. She lives in Vancouver, British Columbia.

The Unshakeable Man in Aldergrove

In Aldergrove a man has a house on the verge
of a view: mountain ranges, shades of blue
craggy peaks flecked with summer snow. In winter
those mountains—he points—are dark blue.
Mount Baker's perennial dollop of icing

changes its colour on evenings,
chameleon to the variables, temperate sky.
I can describe it all
Say that everything here is *like* something else
But today the sky is blue, sky-blue,

flowers bloom, clouds are shaped,
twin engines hum—it's a clear day—eagles eye
tiny dogs they have mistaken for rabbits.
The man in Aldergrove has ambition.
I want to be like those . . . over there (he points) . . .
            mountains.

His wife, she says friends are here
and so the cost of lunch is insignificant
and the day—the sky is blue, sky-blue—is magnificent,
the breeze silk, the silk breeze embracing, breathing
        silk air . . .
it's amazing how things just fit together.

The man with the house on the verge
of two-and-a-half acres in Aldergrove,
pulls up dandelions and mows his lawn before dinner.
During dinner he watches one neighbour's verdant field:
tree-boundaried, dots of silos and barns, flecks of cattle.

There is a hayfield in front of my house, he says,
sloping, silent—it's a hot hot summery day—and
        sprawling,
there is a hayfield between me and my mountains.
But it's not my hayfield, he says, smiling apologetically,
someone else has to cut it.

After dinner the man on the verge
turns up the Gypsy Kings on his tapedeck.
His dogs howl at evening phantoms
and he, relaxed and confident, dances, *chachachacha*,
with his twirling wife, laughing.

Watching the ranges and ranges of mountains
sundown golds, twilight orange, he reflects:
he wishes his life were unshakeable . . .
he gestures, open palm, as if to say, *da-da-da-dum* . . .
unshakeable as a mountain.

Cracks and Crevasses

I

if you can make it there
you can make it . . .

you know how the story goes

but I did not sleep with the city at night;
it is you I miss now I'm gone

I learned about glaciers

by falling into
exploring
the crevice of you

there is a snow coming:
town country city sea-shore look the same
Canada Geese are everywhere

in the heart, in the heat
of night, what is it I know and you don't?

your flight of smile, your weathered
punches

there is a snow coming
and I must leave

leave you before the chill

Waiting

I

They say you're coming,
You'll be here before the fraying of a year—
This time, certain as consequence,
As sea-side dawn and July plum

The boys, the girls
The brass band and the architect
The editor, critic
Home-maker, sushi chef
They're all saying
(Their magnolia assurance infectious)
You're definitely . . . it's confirmed . . . you're coming

I I

I fear it's been said before.
Will I wait again, in vain?
But I bet you knew—
In the past, you would have come and I would have clung
        to my branch
Concerned about all I was lacking

A fruit green enough to chill thought, sour enough to
        shrivel hope

But this time they're shouting it through
The throats of their universe-connected umbilicus

You'll be arriving any day soon, so they're polishing up,
Building towers and treasures and cities and futures
With faxes, pamphlets, plans, determinations

Drum-tight hearts tremble the wait away
They dance, banners above them,
The wind and sun, the auspices of faith,
Rainbow crests bobbing in the sea, they know you're finally
        coming
Light impressing a corner, rounding a corner, a rudder, an
        anchor, the knowing
Sea breeze, moon the length of a day waiting
In a corner, an idea writes a song
The ikebana ladies fillet flowers
The playwright and the conductor
Design poisons and medicines, charms for a storm
There is a group in the basement weaving a banner
With reeds peeled from the muscles of their hearts
A lady on a ladder costumes walls
While someone makes a ruckus with a microphone

In a corridor, in a tower, the choir braids words
Someone uncovers a voice, a color, a note

They polish, they polish
They polish and they polish

Now I feel in my navel the certainty, the pull
Ocean's early tides tossing gifts to the dawn

And this time, this time I'll be a
Star, the sand, night, a full moon
Waiting

III

I've stocked up the refrigerator
There's ice in the icebox
Food in the pot on the stove
I swept
Polished mirrors and made the bed

I'm all dressed up, ready and waiting

Let me know when your plane gets in—
I'll be there, my car tank is full
The tires are pumped, I'm ready to roll

I'm so overwhelmed I fear I'll be unable to talk
So I'll be bringing
The boys and the girls
The brass band and the architect
The editor
The man at the corner store
The hairdresser, the movie buff
The sushi chef and the bookseller

This time, I know you're coming
Only because, this time,
I'm ready, willing, waiting.

Allan Safarik

Allan Safarik has lived the literary life for the past thirty years as a writer, editor, publisher and literary promoter. His books include Okira, The Naked Machine Rides On, God Loves Us Like Earthworks Love Wood, Advertisements for Paradise *and* Vancouver Poetry (*editor*).

Lake of the Moon

Moon below us moving
through the hills
brightness turning gold
back into dust

full moonlight
in the coulees
that wooden match I lit
in the sheltering of your coat
went off like a gunshot

on this hill
a little above the flatlands
in moonlight circumstances
your embracing arms
held my bones together

I gave you a stone
you gave me body of earth
coyotes yapping in the wind
small trees making big
shadowy lunar pictures

Meaning of Time

This morning the sun broke
the porch window pushing
its way into the kitchen
Flowering cherry trees spill
pink joy into windy streets
The confident tap, tapping
of the blind man finding
his way down narrow stairs
becomes inquisitive scratching

He might be asking pavement
for direction or pausing
to inhale the perfumed air
drawing conclusions from the cane's
wiry voice sweeping the bricks
testing every corner of possibility
feeling the sense of the hour
The second hand doesn't stop
travelling for darkness or light

Gregory Scofield

Gregory Scofield is a Metis poet, storyteller, activist and community worker of Cree, Scottish, English and French ancestry. He was born in British Columbia and raised in Saskatchewan, northern Manitoba and the Yukon. He has published four much-praised — and distinctly different — books of poetry: The Gathering: Stones for the Medicine Wheel, *which won the Dorothy Livesay Poetry Prize;* Native Canadiana: Songs from the Urban Rez, *which earned Scofield the Canadian Authors Association Award for Most Promising Young Writer;* Love Medicine and One Song; *and* I Knew Two Metis Women. *He has also published an autobiography,* Thunder Through My Veins: Memories of a Metis Childhood, *with HarperCollins.*

Call Me Brother

"You never know when you're talking to an Indian," he
says wisely because I am only half which we both know
is not the real issue but the way I look which makes it
next to impossible not to spot me sticking out at a
powwow because I have the tourist look that offends
my darker relations who don't see me as related but a
wannabe nuzzling up around the drum to sing 49ers
except I feel the beat like my own heart racing when
curious eyes study if I am just mouthing the words or
actually belting them out because I am a true die-hard
Skin with blue eyes that really screws up the whole
history book image except my roots can't be traced to
the Bering Straight but nine months after European
contact which to this day hasn't been forgiven even
tho we all have some distant grandpa who at one time
or another took an Indian wife which we tend to forget
because anything but pure is less than perfect and we
all secretly need someone to be better than so the
next time you see me up dancing call me brother

Divided

My beigey-pink shade
Unlike you with bronze skin
I'm a Skin without colour; I get the brushoff
Ego-tripping on me again
Deciding if I am pure enough   Red enough
To be whole but the whole of me says
Enough of this colour crap
I am not your white whipping-boy

Growing up in an all-white town
I never forgot my red half   It counted big
Especially if you looked not right white
But wrong white   To white people that's off-white
Dirty white in Sally Ann clothes
You got followed in stores
They just asked a lot if you needed help   Not help
To find the right size but to the door   To the cop shop
If you got caught stealing
That was it   no second chance
They just nailed your raggedy ass to the wall
Never mind in school
You kept your head down   Ducked the put-downs
Shoved it all down

from NATIVE CANADIANA:
SONGS FROM THE URBAN REZ (1996)

1996

I am not ashamed
to admit
I still howl
inconsolably.
The stars too
will be my path
to grandmother moon.
In the dreaming hours
my stones I carry, and
cast
until the last
is shed, and
my feet know the sky.
kaskitêw-makwa / nimâmâ
keeps watch.
My black bear / mother
keeps watch.

kaskitêw-makwa / nimâmâ: my black bear / mother

Snake-dog

iyee   dat one I tinks
between looks   big *skônak*
wants a whole friggin' army
jump into da sack, his hands
wants to rattle me aroun'
shakes me up a bit
for Pete sake   what he tinks
I'm s'posed da crawl over
says hey,
you gots a great *kinêpik* smile
how 'bout slitherin' back
ta my pad
buts I'm no desperate dog
no siree
I wants flute music, horses
a darn good dose
of dat love medicine

iyee: exlamation of disgust or disdain

skônak: female dog; also, a sexually promiscuous person

kinêpik: snake

Treats

I can't remember exactly when
the taste started
only that it came
one night
she grabbed her coat,
told me to wait.

The last time
I hollered, made such a fuss
this time
I wound up tagging along.

Hand in hand
we set out,
down the hill
past the bootlegger's shack,
my hungry eyes
spying for the first time
lonesome alleys, phantom dogs
on midnight streets.

After dark, she said
always walk
in the middle of the road.
And never,
ever get into cars.

Outside the hotel
safely tucked
behind the dumpster
she told me
count to a hundred.
Don't go anywhere,
don't talk to anyone —
just wait.

81, 82, 83
my black bear mother
slight as deer, soft as rabbit
toting her six-pack
slipped into my hand
the salmon jerky treat.

The Poet Leaves A Parting Thought

hâw, ni-nêhiyawêyân and
their English tags behind my every word
word is my rez city lingo
is good enough to get
a bonafide hmm from the white audience
maybe even a raised eyebrow
if I really wow 'em 'n' schmooze 'em
with my dangling modifier talk
in my own Indigenous way
I can be pretty preverbed
when I want

appropriate recognition
I get the usual inconclusive oh
although my buffalo robe talk
can be darn sexy
when I flavour it up with some Cree spice
why waste my breath
on Columbus hot talk
I just end up making him into
a Don Juan hero
as if his slaver descendants
deserve that fame

but it could happen
if I don't give my tongue
a native language mammogram
check it regularly
for English lumps and bumps
I run the chance of becoming
totally anglicized

I wouldn't understand if an elder said
âtayohikî, boy
I'd have to go back to school
for proper instruction

then I'd be just another wannabe book-talker
not an Indigenous oral talker like I am
but a multicultural professor
talker / bragger
bragging how I know up-shot Indians
but what's there to brag about bragging
I don't make 70,000 a year
doing anthropological digs in Peru
more like AIDS studies
because I see these corpses daily
dragging themselves around the city

looking for food or shelter
they just keep popping up
new off the rez
need a place to stay
nowhere to go except Catholic Charities
a transition house
if you're really black 'n' blue
maybe detox
if you've been on an extended bender
I make the appropriate referral
go home scream and write

create dark talk
for white talkers to talk about
I might not be the best
Indigenous poet
but hey, my English is lousy enough
to be honest

hâw, ni-nêhiyawêyân: now, I speak Cree

âtayohikâ: to tell a legned or myth

preverbed: in between a verb and perverted

He Is

earthworm, caterpillar
parting my lips, he is

slug slipping between my teeth
and down, beating

moth wings, a flutter
inside my mouth

he is snail kissing dew
from the shell of my ears,

spider crawling breath tracks
down my neck and weaving

watersnake, he is
swamp frog croaking my chest

hopping from nipple to nipple,
he is mouse

on my belly running circles
and circles, he is

grouse building his nest
from marsh grass and scent,

weasel digging eggs
between my legs,

he is hungry, so hungry
turtle, he is

slow, so slow
nuzzling and nipping

I crack
beneath the weight of him,

he is mountain lion
chewing bones, tasting marrow

rain water
trickling down my spine,

he is spring bear
ample and lean

his berry tongue quick,
sweet from the feasting.

Paskâwêhowi-pîsim

June   The Hatching Moon

Nothing is as it should be.
Moon at my table
is a black wick smoking.
She chokes me on swamp frogs
snickering
to the first sun.
The ducks mind their eggs,
their eyes loose,
loose as snare wire.

Me, I've kissed
the flicker of lizard's tongue.
Now
I want to pluck out his eyes,
pluck out my own
and cast them, all in wailing grief
to the laughing wind.

Nothing is as it should be.
The lake in me is a dry bed
cracking to the bone.
I ache, ache
all that is new

and green and sacred,
all that is reflective of you.

I ache in my smallest bones
but still you won't come
to defend this love.

I curse you
the moon and lizard.
Don't you hear me cracking
bones like wood?
Don't you hear the lullaby
so sweetly red, it bleeds
from the pale stone
splitting my lips?

Nothing is as it should be.
There is only this waiting
and so many songs.

Ceremonies

I heat the stones
between your legs,
my mouth,
the lodge where you come
to sweat.

I fast your lips
commune with spirits,
fly over berry bushes
hungering.

I dance with sun,
float with clouds
your earth smell
deep in my nostrils,
wetting
the tip of my tongue.

I chant with frogs,
sing you to dreams,
bathe you in muskeg,
wrap you in juniper
and sweet pine.

nîcimos, for you
I drink blessed water,
chew the bitter roots
so the medicine is sweet,
the love, sacred.

nîcimos: sweetheart or lover

Not All Halfbreed Mothers

for Mom, Maria

Not all halfbreed mothers

drink

red rose, blue ribbon,
Kelowna Red, Labatt's Blue.

Not all halfbreed mothers
wear cowboy shirts or hats,
flowers behind their ears
or moccasins
sent from up north.

Not all halfbreed mothers
crave wild meat,
settle for hand-fed rabbits
from SuperStore.

Not all halfbreed mothers
pine over lost loves
express their heartache
with guitars, juice harps,
old records shoved
into the wrong dustcover.

Not all halfbreed mothers
read *The Star*, *The Enquirer*,
The Tibetan Book of the Dead
or Edgar Cayce,
know the Lady of Shalott
like she was a best friend
or sister.

Not all halfbreed mothers
speak like a dictionary
or Cree hymn book,
tell stories
about faithful dogs
or bears
that hung around or sniffed
in the wrong place.

Not all halfbreed mothers
know how to saddle
and ride a horse
how to hot-wire a car
or siphon gas.

Not all halfbreed mothers

drink

red rose, blue ribbon,
Kelowna Red, Labatt's Blue.

Mine just happened
to like it

Old Style.

I've Been Told

Halfbreed heaven must be
handmade flowers of tissue,
poplar trees
forever in bloom,

the North and South Saskatchewan rivers
swirling and meeting
like the skirts, the hands
of cloggers
shuffling their moccasined feet.

I've been told

Halfbreed heaven must be
old Gabriel at the gate
calling, "Tawow! Tawow!"
toasting new arrivals, pointing
deportees
to the buffalo jump
or down the Great Canadian Railroad,
like Selkirk or MacDonald.

I've been told

Halfbreed heaven must be
scuffed floors and furniture
pushed to one side,
grannies giggling in the kitchen,
their embroidered hankies
teasing and nudging
the sweetest sweet sixteen,
who will snare the eye
of the best jigger.

I've been told

Halfbreed heaven must be
a wedding party
stretched to the new year,
into a wake, a funeral
then another wedding,
an endless brigade of happy faces
in squeaky-wheeled carts
loaded with accordions, guitars
and fiddles.

I've been told

Halfbreed heaven must be
a rest-over for the Greats:
Hank Williams, Kitty Wells,
The Carter Family
and Hank Snow.

It must be
because I've been told so,

because I know
two Metis women who sing
beyond the blue.

Tawow! Tawow!: Come in, you are welcome!

Mom, As I Watched Her Leaving

became small so very small
as she laboured
her whole eighty pounds
to catch one breath thin as

the sound of my voice
drifting above her,
lost vowels
falling and landing
like snowflakes in a storm,
muted

as the tubes
invading her body, resonating
what was first ingested air,
a wailing song then scream
as the stretch and tear
of my wet head
poked out
and knew by instinct
her language, though frail

and now receding
like the owl
who flutters his wings
beneath her eyes, birthing tears
from a place
beyond my knowing,

beyond the cord which binds me
to those who wait
at the foot of her bed, calling
"Dorothy, peekeewe, peekeewe,"
in a language
I can neither hear nor understand

though each muscle, every cell
of my being
contracts and strains
like the cold fingers
which pull her from my grasp,
struggle
against my every promise.

But in the end, the final moment
I bend to her ear, offer
my own breath
which comes deep and prosperous

sing
my twenty-six years
of memories and songs,
knowing for the first time
life as solitary as death.

And she hears. She hears
as the world closes,
swallows my every vowel,
cuts my every chord releasing

her to a place
where all language
is obsolete.

peekeewe, peekeewe: come home, come home

Dah Ting About Waltzing

is, she said,

never let dah wooman leet

cause if you do

she'll dake yer pants,

make you sign yer cheques

an hant dem over,

push you outta bet

to feet dah babies,

do dah dishes, if she wishes

make you hem her slacks,

go an get flour from dah store

to bake hers a gake,

ice dah damn ting, too.

Best ting, she said,

are dah ones

who step on yer does.

Sandy Shreve

Sandy Shreve was raised in Sackville, New Brunswick and now lives in Vancouver BC where she works as Communications Coordinator for the Legal Services Society. Previously she worked for more than eight years as Departmental Assistant for the Women's Studies Department at Simon Fraser University; earlier jobs include: reporter, library assistant, secretary. Sandy founded and coordinated Poetry in Transit, displaying poems in BC Transit Sky Train cars and buses. Her books of poetry are Belonging (*Sono Nis Press, 1997; shortlisted for the Milton Acorn People's Poetry Award*), Bewildered Rituals (*Polestar Book Publishers, 1992*) *and* The Speed of the Wheel Is Up to the Potter (*Quarry Press, 1990*).

Spring Cleaning

weeding the files I pretend
the cabinet into a plot of land
as if through this thinning
it will blossom
and everyone who walks in
will admire my new bouquet
lean into each drawer
and breathe deeply the scent
of sorted papers, no longer
ragged edges crammed in every
which way and poised to slash
at skin in vengeance
but petal soft and quivering
to the gentle nudge
of noses seeking fragrance
instead of sneezing dust
now billowing up as I shred
pile after pile of paper
bound for some recycling bin
and bound to come back to me

again in more superfluous copies
to be stuffed and wedged and jammed
into the spaces I've created
for flowers

Snow Sestina

for Maggie Benston

The mountain doffs its cap of cloud
to the dazzling art of snow
and standing here with all this in my eyes
I breathe in several degrees below
zero, up to my knees in powder
a breeze caressing my face

I cannot begin to fill my eyes
with the clarity of winter air   Here below
the sudden frescoes of snow
miles distant, I feel face to face
with those sweeping strokes of powder
paintings, fallen from a cloud

This morning sounds like powder
floating in the air   Just below
the stillness of a willow cloaked in snow
I bend to form an angel out of cloud
that's landed here to cool my face
and tantalize my eyes

It sparkles crystalline, this eau de snow
melting on my mitten, scents my face
the one perfume I'll wear, a dab of cloud
here, on my forehead, neck and just below
each ear, each touch as soft as powder
puffs, swift as the blink of eyes

The beauty of geometry in snow
is like a poem and the grin on your face
when I said I loved the math in words—cloud
covered thoughts unveiled like equations, eyes
opened to shifting solutions, below
above and around each phrase, whimsical as powder
in a wind, images and ideas to create, then face
and balance as best I can—the way snow
can be both flurry and blizzard, powder
and firm, a pleasure to the eyes
and agony for skin, glowering in a pewter cloud
while lighting up night on the ground below

The mountains flaunt white powder, while below
city dwellers' eyes are on the sky, dread any cloud
that delivers more snow than we know how to face

Dulse

tastes just this side of bitter
paper thin and purple, I savour
its salt-air flavour
much to my husband's disgust
how can you eat that stuff!
my fishy kisses
greeted with suspicion
so I exile myself
to the opposite side of the room
defiantly feast
on an insignificant cultural gap
vast as a continent
between us

Tom Wayman

Tom Wayman's most recent books are a collection of his poems, The Colours of the Forest *(Harbour, 1999) and an anthology of contemporary Canadian love poems,* The Dominion of Love *(Harbour, 2001). When not teaching in BC's community college system, he is the Squire of "Appledore," his estate in the Selkirk Mountains near Nelson, British Columbia.*

Getting The News

At her words, the small boy inside me
is shoved face forward
trips, hits gravel
and begins to slide
Palms and knees tear open
the flesh peels back
like flames shrivelling paper
Grains of rock embed themselves
in the expanding cuts
so when I coast to a stop
in a blur of pain
and stand shakily erect
I attempt only once to brush clear
skinned flesh:
my blunt hands
force gravel further into my wounds
Alone on the road
my hurts filming over with blood

I swallow air
ready to howl my agony
swallow air
air

The Politics of the House: Tables

Tables are egalitarians.
Each stands on its four legs
and whatever is placed on them—a sumptuous cloth
and silver cutlery
or a paper cover with plastic plates and spoons—
the table knows its purpose is the same.
Even the most exquisitely carved sorts
are cautioned by their parents when young:
Never forget: take our chairs away from us
and all we are is a shelf.
But as long as we bear up
those objects we are asked to hold
we are each successfully doing our work in the world.

In this way tables are like horses:
indifferent to whether they carry a rich man
on an expensive saddle
or a young girl bareback, pull a plough
or a carriage of tourists. Certain kinds of horses
are best for specific jobs
but among horses themselves there are no hierarchies.
A Clydesdale believes itself as accomplished in its own way
as an Arabian, neither one deferring to
nor lording it over the other.

Unlike horses, though,
tables remain of human civilization:
a central item of our houses—kitchen table,
sewing table—and our cities
—workbench, packing table.
Sadly, the men and women around the boardroom table
still imagine themselves worth more
than the women and men seated at the lunchroom tables
on their break. Yet in the midst
of all our ranking and gradations,
qualifications, certificates, and ornate hats,
tables
patiently continue to demonstrate
the ubiquitous nature of equality.

The Grave of Literary Ambition

I was planting bulbs on the grave
where literary ambition
is buried. Why not, I reasoned,
honour with beauty
the final resting place
of the friend/enemy
who sustained me for years?
I dug a shallow trench
and placed clusters of daffodils
and then tulips: each of these bulbs
the size and feel of a cooking onion.
Next I sowed crocuses, to provide a contrasting
purple shade
below the higher-stemmed, brighter flowers.
Then I sifted soil
to cover what I planted
and as the instructions on the bulb packages advised
spread a coating of leaves for mulch.

But as I gathered
my shovel and rake and hoses
and was putting them in the wheelbarrow
I noticed a green shoot
poking through the brown layer of leaves.

"Must be the unseasonal weather,
warm for November,"
I thought, "or else my old ambition
is a powerful fertilizer.
Of course, maybe one bulb
is a hyperactive mutant."
Before I could trundle the barrow away,
however, another shoot appeared. And a third.
Suddenly dozens were springing up
everywhere on the low mound.
And the first one
already was producing
a tightly furled growth at its tip.
Within about a minute,
as more green spear-points
stabbed upward amid the leaves,
it unfolded a gorgeous,
multi-hued
petal-soft
letter A.
Seconds later, more flower-letters
opened—not in any particular order—
to the autumn breeze
until the grave was transformed into a swaying,
iridescent

alphabet soup
lifted atop thick stalks.

Then the growth ended.
The letters waited
under a grey sky.
I picked a number of consonants and vowels
at random
and after I returned my gardening tools to the shed
I stuck the letters in a vase on my desk.

When I look up from my pen
or keyboard
here they are. Yet at idle moments
I catch myself starting a list
of words
that can be formed from these flowers.

Dale Zieroth

Dale Zieroth's sixth book of poems is Crows Do Not Have Retirement *(Harbour Publishing, 2001). He won the Dorothy Livesay Poetry Prize for his fifth book,* How I Joined Humanity at Last *(Harbour, 1998). He has also published two chapbooks:* The Tangled Bed *(Reference West, 2000) and* Palominos and other poems *(Gasperau Press, 2000). His poems have been nominated for a National Magazine Award, and have appeared in more than thirty-five anthologies, including* A Matter of Spirit: Recovery of the Sacred in Contemporary Canadian Poetry *(Ekstasis, 1998).*

from THE WEIGHT OF
MY RAGGEDY SKIN (1991)

On Or About Midnight

. . . the tall lamplight
creeps palely down to blanch the grass
and send thin roots
into Mosquito Creek Lane
where my daughter walks.

Off the bus and through
the Buy-Low parking lot for pale light
from scattered, buzzing poles
beneath which she hurries,
girl in the dark.

Later if we share pink lemonade
In a few words we see
I have not kept pace
with her own will
to keep harm away.

Her speed I remember then,
the quick dancer's legs
and how they can leap, bend
and challenge.

But when she next is gone
I remember, too, the malignant grass
along which she must run.

Three Wishes

That I may grow
another room (hidden from all)
into which I step and leave behind
where the neighbourhood
skateboards prowl
and the citizens
writhing sea to sea
write their MPs.

For my neighbour:
that he might hold his rearview
mirror less lovingly
as he wipes his car today;
that he directs himself away
from mechanization and
spin inward, elsewhere
and come to greet me then;
that we could speak, and I perhaps
would know him better.

I travel to work
and I see from the train
a man working construction below.
I cannot see his face,

he is only inches tall,
his arms held high in the air hour after hour
receiving loads of steel
from the cranes above.
I wish him to be
an archangel of happiness toward which
the burden of our hearts may start to flow.

David Dale

Forced to abandon him
by a grade one teacher who could not accept
two boys with the same name, I accepted
my second. I think of David
as a skin dropped, a ball
lost in the summer grass.

My parents often spoke of him
or mouthed my new name
as if I were a guest
and they were waiting politely
for his return

—because what faults I had
could never spring from him.
Well, did he grow up
through change, embarrassment,
and try to speak the lines
reserved after all for him? He never did.

When I meet him now
at dawn or just before sleep, he stands
speechless although I know he wants from me
more than words.

Lately, when I cut myself
on paper, and the sharp red line wells over
and falls, his young mouth
is pressed against my hand.

INDEX *of titles or first lines*

BRIGHT LIGHTS *from* POLESTAR BOOK PUBLISHERS

Polestar takes pride in creating books that enrich our understanding of the world, and in introducing superb writers to discriminating readers.

Recent and Forthcoming Fiction:

Pool-Hopping and Other Stories by Anne Fleming

Shortlisted for the Governor-General's Award, the Ethel Wilson Fiction Prize and the Danuta Gleed Award. "Fleming's evenhanded, sharp-eyed and often hilarious narratives traverse the frenzied chaos of urban life with ease and precision." — *The Georgia Straight*
1-896095-18-6 $16.95 CAN / $13.95 USA

What's Left Us by Aislinn Hunter

Six stories and an unforgettable novella by a prodigiously talented writer. "Aislinn Hunter is a gifted writer with a fresh energetic voice and a sharp eye for the detail that draws you irresistibly into the intimacies of her story." — Jack Hodgins
1-55192-412-9 $21.95 CAN / $15.95 USA

Daughters are Forever by Lee Maracle

Maracle's new novel reinforces her status as one of the most important First Nations writers. A moving story about First Nations people in the modern world and the importance of courage, truth and reconciliation.
1-55192-410-2 $21.95 CAN / $16.95 USA

diss/ed banded nation by David Nandi Odhiambo

"Thoroughly convincing in its evocation of young, rebellious, impoverished urban lives ... an immersion into a simmering stew of racial and cultural identities ..."— *The Globe and Mail* 1-896095-26-7 $16.95 CAN / $13.95 USA

Stubborn Bones by Karen Smythe

"Karen Smythe brings to her fiction a combination of sharp intelligence and delicate sensibility. With a few deft strokes she manages, in these understated stories, to create a mood—lyrical and elegaic—that haunts the reader long after the book is finished."
—*Joan Givner*
1-55192-364-5 $21.95 CAN / $1695 USA

Some Girls Do by Teresa McWhirter

This is a rare kind of novel: a genuinely revelatory portrait of a generation rarely described in fiction. In prose that's as sharp as broken glass and shot through with bolts of poetry, Teresa McWhirter unlocks the extraordinary sub-culture of urban adults in their twenties.
1-55192-495-5 $21.95 CAN / $15.95 USA